Kidnapped

Introduction

Robert Louis Stevenson was born in 1850, in Edinburgh, Scotland. After studying law at Edinburgh University, he decided to earn his living as a writer. Unfortunately, he became ill with tuberculosis, a disease of the lungs, and he had to travel to warmer countries to improve his health.

In 1880, Robert Louis Stevenson married Fanny Osborne and a year later, he wrote *Treasure Island* for her young son. In 1886, *Kidnapped* was published. Both these books were very popular, but they did not make much money. So, in 1886, Stevenson wrote *The Strange Case of Dr Jekyll and Mr Hyde*. This story made Stevenson well known, and made him more money, because it was bought by adults.

Kidnapped is a story of the kidnapping of David Balfour, a young boy who is cheated out of his inheritance and wrongly accused of murder. It is set in 1751, five years after the Jacobites (led by Bonnie Prince Charlie, the son of James II) were defeated at Culloden Moor in the north of Scotland. The Jacobites supported James II, who claimed the right to be the king of Great Britain, instead of King George. Most of the Scottish Highlanders were loyal Jacobites and had their land taken from them by King George.

In 1887, Stevenson's father died. With the money he left, Robert Louis Stevenson and his family were able to live in Samoa, an island in the Pacific Ocean. The warm climate improved his health and he wrote there until his death in 1894.

You might find the meaning of these words will help you to understand the story better:

ay(e)	yes
brae	hill
burn	stream
clan	group of families with the same family name
crofter	a farmer
dirk	dagger
Gaelic	a Celtic language
glen	mountain valley
The Highlands	a large area of north and north-east Scotland
Jacobite	a supporter of James Stuart who wanted to rule Britain
ken	know
laird	a Scottish landowner
loch	lake
The Lowlands	the central and eastern part of Scotland
nae	no, not
Redcoats	British soldiers (they wore scarlet jackets)
ye	you

CHAPTER ONE
The House of Shaws

The story of kidnap and murder that you are about to read began one June morning in 1751. I was only seventeen and both my parents had just died. I decided to leave Essendean, the village where I had always lived, and seek my fortune in the world. The minister of Essendean, Mr Campbell, came to see me before I left.

"I have something for ye, lad," he said. "When your father was ill, he gave this letter to me. Ye are to take it to the house of Shaws, near Edinburgh."

I looked at him in surprise.

"The Balfours of Shaws is an old and respected family – your family," he told me. "That is where your father came from and he wanted you to go back there."

He gave me the letter addressed in my father's handwriting:

> *To Ebenezer Balfour, Esquire,*
> *the house of Shaws*
> *to be delivered by my son, David Balfour*

"Remember, Davie," Mr Campbell said, "that Ebenezer Balfour is the laird and you must obey him."

"I'll try, sir," I said.

"Now you must go," Mr Campbell said sadly, "you have two days walking ahead of you."

I took my last look at the churchyard where my mother and father were buried, then I began my journey. How pleased I was to be leaving the quiet countryside to go to a great and busy house, among rich people of my own family!

In the middle of the second day, I caught sight of the sea from the top of a hill – and the great city of Edinburgh. I was very excited, but when I started to ask the way to the house of Shaws, people looked at me in surprise.

"If ye'll take my advice," one man said sharply, "ye'll keep away from the Shaws."

At first, I wanted to turn back.

"No!" I told myself firmly, "now that I've come so far, I have to find out for myself."

Just as the sun began to set, I met an old woman trudging down a hill.

"Am I far from the house of Shaws?" I asked her.

She took me back up the hill and pointed to the valley below.

"That is the house of Shaws!" she said angrily. "Blood built it. Blood stopped the building of it. Blood will be its ruin. I spit upon the ground and curse Ebenezer Balfour!"

I was frightened by her words, but I forced myself to walk up to the house. The nearer I got, the gloomier it seemed. There was no gate and no avenue - and one wing of the house was unfinished. Was this the fine house my father was sending me to? Was this where I was going to earn my fortune?

I knocked once on the wooden door. There was silence. I waited and knocked again. Then I felt angry and shouted, "Mr Balfour! Mr Ebenezer Balfour!" until a man called from the bedroom window above my head.

"It's loaded."

I looked up into the mouth of a gun.

"I've come here with a letter," I said, "to Mr Ebenezer Balfour of the house of Shaws. Is he here?"

"Ye can put it down upon the doorstep, and be off with ye," the man said.

"No!" I cried. "I will deliver it into Mr. Balfour's hands. It is a letter of introduction. I am David Balfour."

There was a long pause.

"Is your father dead?" the man asked at last.

I was too upset to answer.

"Ay," the man said, "he'll be dead. I'll let you in."

After a few minutes, a stooping man of about fifty opened the door. His face was grey and mean, and he had a long beard trailing onto his nightshirt. He led me down a corridor to a cold, dark kitchen.

"Let me see the letter," he said.

"It's for Mr Balfour," I answered.

"And who do ye think I am?" he said. "Now give me Alexander's letter."

"You know my father's name?" I asked in surprise.

"It would be strange if I didnae," the man said, "for he was my younger brother."

"I never knew, sir, that he had a brother," I said, my voice trembling.

I slept badly that night, locked in a cold bedroom with broken window-panes, but the next day my uncle seemed friendlier. In the evening, when we had eaten some porridge together, he lit a pipe and leaned towards me across the table.

"Davie, my man," he said, "I'm going to help ye as your father wanted. I kept a bit of money for ye, since ye were born – not much – well, forty pounds!"

I was too surprised to say anything.

"I want nae thanks," he said. "I do my duty. But I want ye to do something for me. There's a chest in the tower at the far end of the house, the part that's not finished. Bring it down for me."

"Can I have a candle, sir?" I asked.

"Nae lights in my house," he told me.

I went outside. It was darker than ever. My heart pounded as I climbed the steps to the top of the tower, feeling the wall with my hands. Suddenly, there was a flash of lightning and I looked down in horror. The unfinished staircase came to an end there, high in the air.

"One more step and I would have fallen!" I gasped.

Then the terrible thought came into my mind.

"My uncle sent me here to die!"

CHAPTER TWO
Kidnapped!

I came slowly down the steps again and went back to the kitchen. When I crept up behind my uncle and put my hands on his shoulders, he fell to the floor like a dead man.

"Sit up!" I shouted.

"Are ye alive?" my uncle sobbed. "O man. Are ye alive?"

"I am," I said, "no thanks to you. Why did you try to kill me?"

"I'll talk to ye in the morning," my uncle moaned, "I feel too ill right now."

I locked my uncle in his room. Then I lit the biggest fire the house had seen for years and fell asleep. In the morning, as I was deciding what to do, a ship's boy called Ransome brought a letter for my uncle.

"It's from Captain Hoseason," my uncle said. "He's just sailed into Queensferry port. He wants to see me."

I shook my head.

"I've treated ye badly, Davie," he said. "If ye let me see the captain, I'll take ye to see my lawyer, Mr Rankeillor in Queensferry. He knew your father. We'll sort out some money for ye."

"I do want to see the sea," I thought. "I'll go, but I won't let my uncle out of my sight."

We followed Ransome to an inn alongside the port. The room where my uncle and Hoseason talked was so hot that I left them for a few minutes to look at the ships. When I returned, my uncle was coming downstairs with Captain Hoseason.

"Ye shall come on board my ship for half-an-hour," the captain smiled, "just until the tide comes in, and have a drink with me."

"No thank you," I said, "we're on our way to see Mr Rankeillor."

"I know that," the captain said, "and I can stop at Queensferry pier, a stone's throw from the lawyer's house." He bent over and whispered in my ear. "Be careful of your uncle, he's a cunning old fox. Perhaps I can help ye."

I thought I had found a friend.

We went over to the ship in a rowing boat. I boarded the ship first with the captain and waited for my uncle to come on board. There was no sign of him.

"Where's my uncle?" I asked at last.

The captain did not answer. I looked down at the rowing boat below and saw my uncle rowing back to the shore. I shouted, "Help! Help!" until I felt a hard blow on the back of my head. Then I fell down onto the deck.

When I came round again, I was lying in the pitch black, tied up and in great pain. I heard the roaring of the sea, the thundering of the sails and the shouts of the seamen. My whole world heaved up and down. I trembled with fear and despair. I did not know whether it was night or day in that evil-smelling ship where rats pattered across my face.

"They've kidnapped me!" I whispered to myself.

I think I would have died if the second officer, Mr Riach, had not taken me up on the deck. In the fresh air, I began to feel better. I told Mr Riach what had happened.

"I will do my best to help ye, lad," he said. "But ye're not the only one this has happened to."

"Where are we?" I asked.

"Between the Orkney and the Shetland Islands," he told me. "In a few days, we'll be going round the north coast of Scotland."

"Then where?" I whispered.

"America," Mr Riach replied.

I slowly began to feel stronger and I began to think of ways to escape. But as that became less and less likely, I imagined what my new life would be like if I was a slave in a strange country. About a week later, the captain came looking for me.

"Davie, lad," he said kindly, "we want ye to go and

work up in the roundhouse instead of Ransome."

"But what about Ransome?" I asked, jumping out of my bunk.

As I spoke, a man put Ransome in my bunk. I looked at the boy's white face and my blood ran cold. I knew that he was dead.

The roundhouse stood six feet high above the ship's deck. Inside were bunks for the captain, Mr Riach and Mr Shuan, the first officer. Most of the food and drink and guns were also kept here. Light came from a small skylight. I listened as I served these men, and I learned that it was Mr Shuan who had beaten poor Ransome to death.

On the tenth day after my kidnapping, near the Hebrides, we sailed into a thick, white fog. At ten o' clock that evening, there was a loud noise.

"We've hit something!" the captain yelled.

We all rushed to the side of the ship and looked down. We had cut a small boat in two. Only one man had escaped by clinging to the bow of our ship. We pulled him aboard and took him to the roundhouse.

The stranger was small and nimble. His sunburnt face was freckled and pitted with smallpox scars. When he took off his overcoat, he took a pair of pistols from the pockets and laid them on the table. A fine sword hung from his belt. His clothes were elegant – a feathered hat, black velvet breeches and a blue, silver-buttoned coat edged with lace.

"I was on my way to France," the stranger said. "If ye can take me there, I'll pay ye well."

"Ye've a French soldier's coat upon your back, and a Scottish tongue in your head," the captain said. "Are ye a Jacobite?"

"Are ye?" the stranger asked.

"No!" the captain answered sternly, "not me. I'm for King George."

"Will ye take me to France?" the stranger asked again.

"No," the captain said, "but I can take ye back to where ye came from."

"Very well," the stranger said. "I'll give ye well if ye take me to Loch Linnhe."

They shook hands and Captain Hoseason went onto the deck to tell his men. I stood alone with the stranger, my heart beating with excitement. I had heard many stories of exiled Jacobites coming back to Scotland from France to fetch money from their supporters in the Highlands. Was this man one of them standing right in front of me with a belt of golden guineas around his waist?

"Are you a Jacobite?" I asked him.

"Ay," he said. "And are ye for King George?"

"I don't know," I said, not wanting to annoy him.

"Bring me some more wine," the Jacobite said, holding out an empty bottle.

I left the roundhouse to fetch the key for the store room. As I came closer to the captain and his men, I felt that something was wrong. I crept up behind them and listened.

"We'll kill the Jacobite and…" the captain stopped speaking as I stepped forward.

"Captain," I said, "will you give me the key to the store room?"

"Now, Davie," Mr Riach said, "that Jacobite Highlander in there is the enemy of King George. I want ye to bring out a pistol or two for us."

I made my way slowly back to the roundhouse. What should I do? These seamen were cruel thieves. They had kidnapped me from my own country. They had killed poor Ransome. Now they would kill the Jacobite stranger. What if I helped him?

I went into the roundhouse and stared at the Jacobite. And there and then, I made up my mind.

"They're all murderers on this ship!" I cried. "Now it's your turn!"

"My name is Alan Breck of the house of Stewart," he said quickly. "Will ye fight with me, lad?"

"I'm not a thief or a murderer – I'm David Balfour, of the house of Shaws. Yes, I'll fight with you!" I said.

CHAPTER THREE
The Siege of the Roundhouse

"Your job is to watch the door," Alan said. "If they try to open it, ye shoot. Climb on the bed and watch the window at the same time. How many are they?"

"Fifteen," I told him.

Alan whistled in surprise. By now, the captain and his men were tired of waiting for me to come back with the guns. Suddenly, Captain Hoseason appeared in the doorway. Alan pointed his sword at him.

"The sooner we fight, the sooner ye'll feel this sword through your body!" he cried.

The captain said nothing to Alan, but gave me an ugly look.

"I'll remember this, Davie lad," he said.

The next moment, he had gone. Alan pulled out a dirk with his left hand.

"Keep your head," he said, "for there's no going back now, lad."

I climbed up to the window, clutching a handful of pistols. My heart was beating like a bird's, faintly and quickly. I felt no hope, only an anger against the world. The attack came all of a sudden – a rush of feet, a roar, a shout from Alan, then the clash of swords as he fought with Mr Shuan.

"He killed Ransome!" I shouted.

"Watch the window!" Alan shouted back.

As he spoke, he plunged his sword into Shuan's body.

I looked through the window and saw five men running past with a large piece of wood. They tried to break down the door with it. I took a deep breath and fired at them. I must have hit one of them because the other four stopped running. I shot twice more and they ran away. Now the roundhouse was full of smoke from my pistols. Alan stood waiting, his sword covered with blood.

Suddenly, more men rushed against the door. At the same time, the glass of the skylight shattered and a man leaped through. I was too afraid to shoot. I hit him over the back of the head with a pistol but he tried to grab hold of me. My courage came back and I shot him. Then I shot another man at the skylight and he fell on top of his friend.

There were more men in the doorway. Alan's sword flashed, and every flash was followed by a man's scream, until the rest of the men ran away. Alan pushed the four dead seamen out of the roundhouse with his sword.

I could hardly breathe. The sight of the two men I had shot flashed in front of me like a nightmare. I began to sob like a child.

"Ye're a brave lad, David," Alan said kindly, "and I love ye like a brother. Sleep now. I'll take the first watch."

In the morning, Alan cut one of the silver buttons from his coat.

"I give ye this for last night's work," he said. "And wherever ye show this button, the friends of Alan Breck will help ye."

As he finished speaking, Mr Riach called out to us.

"The Captain wants to speak to the Jacobite!"

Alan went over to the window.

"Take me to Loch Linnhe as we agreed!" Alan called out angrily.

"Ay," Hoseason said, "but my Shuan is dead, thanks to ye two. None of us ken this dangerous coast, like he did. Can ye show us the way?"

"I'm more of a fighting man than a sailorman," Alan answered, "but I ken something of this land. I'll help ye."

We exchanged a bottle of brandy for two buckets of water, and the meeting came to an end. Alan and I sat all day long, exchanging stories. To my amazement, he told me that he had joined the British army because he had no money. He had later deserted and joined the Jacobites.

"Dear, oh dear," I said, "the punishment for desertion is death. Why have you come back to Scotland? Have you come to collect money?"

"I miss my friends and my country," Alan sighed. "I want to see the heather and the deer. But ye guess right, Davie. I'm here to collect money for Ardshiel, the captain of my clan. He fled to France when the Jacobites were beaten at the battle of Culloden. His Highland crofters now have to pay rent to King George, but they still send rent to Ardshiel."

"They pay their rent twice!" I said in surprise. "How loyal they must be!"

I told Alan a little about myself, and how Mr

Campbell had given me my father's letter.

"I would do nothing to help a Campbell," Alan said angrily. "They've fought my clan for many years, and taken their land. I hate Colin Campbell more than all the others. We call him the Red Fox because of his red hair …"

Alan stopped for a moment as if he were too angry to speak.

"When Ardshiel fled to France," Alan continued, "Red Fox asked King George if he could collect the rent for Ardshiel's land. Now he's slowly getting rid of all Ardshiel's crofters. If ever I have the time to hunt him down, I…"

Alan said no more.

We didn't talk about it again that day. Later that night, under a cold and clear sky, the ship struck some rocks. The sea came over the deck and we could hear the ship breaking up under our feet.

"Where are we?" I shouted to Alan above the roaring waves.

"Off the coast of Mull," he shouted back. "Campbell country."

Before I could speak again, an enormous wave lifted the ship up and threw me into the sea.

CHAPTER FOUR
The Murder of Red Fox

I do not know how many times I sank under the water. Just as I thought I would drown, I caught hold of a piece of wood. Soon, I floated into calmer water. Then, by kicking my legs, I came to the shore. And here I began the most unhappy part of my adventures.

As soon as it was morning, I climbed to the top of a hill and looked out to sea. I could not see the ship or my shipmates. I was on a small island, close to the Island of Mull. I started to walk across the island, looking for a way to get across to Mull itself.

On the second day, a fishing boat passed by, and the men on it shouted to me in Gaelic and laughed. Two days later, it came back and the men pointed towards Mull. At last, I understood.

"They're telling me I can walk to Mull when the tide is out," I thought. "How stupid I've been!"

I set off as soon as the tide was out. As soon as I reached the mainland, I came across an old gentleman, smoking his pipe in the sun.

"Have you seen any men from the ship out there?" I asked. "One of them was dressed like a gentleman."

He shook his head.

"Was there one with a feathered hat?" I asked again.

He shook his head again.

"Are ye the lad with the silver button?" he asked at last.

"Why, yes!" I cried in surprise.

"Then I have a message for ye," he said. "Ye are to follow your friend to his country, to Appin."

I walked almost a hundred miles in the next four days, asking the way from everyone I met. At last, I came to the other side of Mull where I took a ferry over to the Scottish mainland. The boatman was called Neil Roy, one of Alan's clan, and I was keen to talk to him.

"I'm looking for somebody," I said. "Alan Breck Stewart's his name."

"The man you ask for is in France," Neil answered.

I remembered the silver button and showed it to him in the palm of my hand.

"Ye might have shown me the button straight away," he said. "But now all is well. I have been told to see that ye are safe."

I travelled on, remembering Neil Roy's advice – to speak to no one on the way, to avoid the Redcoats, and to hide in the bushes if any of them came. At last I came to the banks of Loch Linnhe.

I asked a fisherman to take me across the loch. Although it was only noon when we set out, the sky was dark, and the mountains around us were black and gloomy. On the other side of the loch, I sat thinking for a while.

"Am I doing the right thing?" I asked myself, "going to join an outlaw like Alan?"

Suddenly, four men came into view on the steep path below me – a large, red-headed gentlemen, a lawyer wearing a white wig, a servant and a sheriff's officer. I stepped out of the heather.

"Can you tell me the way to Appin?" I called to them.

They all stared at me in surprise.

"Who are ye looking for there?" the man with the red hair asked me.

"That's my business, sir," I told him.

As the man opened his mouth to reply, a shot came from the hill above me and he fell from his horse.

"I am dying! I am dying!" he cried.

I stared for a moment in horror. Then I ran up the hill, crying out, "Murderer! Murderer!" In the distance, I caught sight of a tall man in a black coat.

"Up here!" I shouted. "I can see him! Come up here! He's getting away!"

As I waited, a group of Redcoats came along the road.

"Ten pounds if ye take the lad!" the lawyer shouted to them. "He has helped to murder Colin Campbell."

Red Fox! Alan Breck's greatest enemy! My heart

started to pound loudly. I stood frozen to the spot as I watched the soldiers spread out in the woods below me and raise their guns.

"Hide here," a man's voice whispered.

In the shelter of the trees I found Alan Breck.

CHAPTER FIVE
Journey to the Lowlands

Alan began to run through the trees and I followed him. Then we crawled through the heather. We couldn't stop and my heart seemed to be bursting against my ribs. I had no time to think, no breath to talk. A quarter of an hour later, Alan stopped and lay flat in the heather.

"Do as I do," he told me. "Your life depends on it."

Now we crawled back the way we had come, until we came to the wood where I had first found him. He lay, face down, in the bracken and panted like a dog. I lay beside him as if I were dead.

Alan was the first to get up. At first, I said nothing. The man that Alan hated was dead. And here was Alan hiding in the woods, running from the soldiers. Was my only friend in that wild country guilty?

"You and me cannot stay together," I told him angrily. "I like you very well, Alan, but your ways are not mine, and they're not God's. We must part."

"I'll not part from ye, David," Alan said, "until ye give me good reason. If ye ken something I don't, tell me."

"Alan," I said. "You know very well that Colin Campbell lies dead on the road down there."

"Did ever ye hear the story of the Man and the Good People?" Alan asked.

At last, Alan stopped under an enormous rock. He climbed to the top, pulling me after him, and we lay flat, looking all around us. It was a clear dawn and we could see the stony sides of the valley. There were no houses anywhere, and it was silent except for the eagles screeching around the mountain tops. Alan smiled.

"Now we have a chance," he said. "Ye're not very good at this jumping, are ye, David?"

I blushed.

"No blame to ye!" he laughed. "You did what ye were afraid of. That's the best kind of man. And I'm to blame for having nae water with us, only brandy!"

"Empty out the brandy," I said, "then I'll go down to the river and fill the bottle."

Alan shook his head.

"I wouldnae waste it," he said. "Now sleep, lad, I'll keep watch."

I woke up at about nine in the morning. It was cloudless and very hot.

"Ye were snoring," Alan told me, his face anxious.

"Does that matter?" I asked.

"Ay, it does," he said. "Look down there."

I peered over the edge of the rock and gasped in surprise. About half-a-mile up the river was a Redcoat camp. On the top of a rock stood a sentry and there were other sentries all along the river. In the distance were soldiers on horse-back.

"This is what I was afraid of, Davie," Alan said. "They're watching the burn-side. We'll try to get past them tonight."

"And what are we to do until then?" I asked.

"Hide here," he said.

We lay on top of that rock, like scones baking over a fire. The little patch of earth and fern was only big enough for one, so we took turns to lie there. We had no water, but we kept the brandy as cool as we could.

And all this time the soldiers made their way along the valley towards us, prodding the heather with their bayonets. My blood ran cold at the sight of them. Then they started to climb the slopes of the mountain. Suddenly, there were soldiers all around the bottom of our rock as they sat down to rest.

I almost stopped breathing with fear.

CHAPTER SEVEN
Wanted: Dead or Alive

We lay there for two hours. It was only luck and the hot sun that saved us.

"We should go now," Alan whispered at last, "while they're asleep."

We slipped from one rock to the other, crawling flat on our bellies, then making a run for it. Most of the soldiers, still sleepy in the sun, stayed down by the river. We slowly got away from them, although we could still see the sentry on the rock.

At last we came to a burn and plunged ourselves into its cool water. Then we mixed oatmeal with it and ate – a good enough dish for a hungry man.

We moved on quickly again that night. It was a difficult path – up the sides of high mountains and along steep cliffs. I was afraid all the time. It was still dark when we reached our destination – a cleft in the great mountain with water running through it. There were caves and woods and trout in the stream. We even dared to light a fire. It was here that Alan taught me how to use a sword.

"We've been here for five days," Alan said one day. "I must send word to James. Could ye lend me my button,

Davie?"

I gave him the silver button. He tied it to a little cross of twigs.

"There's a friend of mine living not far from here – John Breck," he said, "and I can trust him with my life. Ye see, David, there will be a reward for us now, dead or alive. So I cannae show my face, even to go to my friends. But when it's dark, I'll leave my silver button."

"And what will John Breck do when he finds it?" I asked.

"In our clan, this cross is the signal for a meeting," he told me, "but since there's no letter with it, he kens that cannae be. But he will ken there is something wrong. When he sees my button, he'll think, 'Alan Breck is in the heather, and has need of me.'"

"But there's a great deal of heather," I said. "How will he find us?"

"True," Alan answered, "but then he'll see the birch and the pine twigs, and he'll ken where to come."

"Would it not be simpler to write?" I asked.

"That is an excellent idea, Mr Balfour of Shaws," Alan said, "it certainly would be simpler. But it would be very difficult for John Breck to read it. He would have to go to school to learn first."

That night, Alan placed his cross in John Breck's window. About noon the next day, we saw a man coming up the side of the mountain, guided by Alan's whistling. John Breck was a ragged, bearded man, with terrible smallpox scars on his face. He took Alan's message and left straight away.

It was three days before John Breck came back. He brought bad news – everybody was saying that Alan had murdered Colin Campbell, the countryside was alive with Redcoats looking for him and James Stewart was already in prison accused of helping in the murder.

"Can it get any worse?" Alan asked.

John Breck unrolled a poster sent by James's wife.

WANTED:

A SMALL MAN, POCK-MARKED
SKIN, OF ABOUT THIRTY-FIVE, DRESSED IN
A FEATHERED HAT, A FRENCH COAT OF
BLUE WITH SILVER BUTTONS AND LACE,
A RED WAISTCOAT AND BREECHES OF BLACK
VELVET. HE IS WITH A TALL STRONG LAD OF
ABOUT EIGHTEEN, WEARING A RAGGED
BLUE COAT, AN OLD HIGHLAND BONNET,
A LONG WAISTCOAT, BLUE BREECHES, BARE
LEGS, HEAVY SHOES WITH HOLES AT THE
TOES, SPEAKS LIKE A LOWLANDER, AND
HAS NO BEARD.

Then John Breck took out his purse and took out four guineas in gold, and another in small change.

"I thank ye," Alan said, putting the coins in his pocket. "And now, John Breck, if ye will hand over my button, we'll be off again."

Eleven hours of hard travelling over a range of high mountains brought us right to the edge of a wide moor. Alan looked at me, his face pale and worried.

"It's not a good place, Davie, lad," he said, "but we have to cross it."

CHAPTER EIGHT

Escape across the Moor

As we stood there, the mist rose away from the moor and showed us the countryside we had to cross. Most of it was red with heather and some was blackened by fire. Here and there, it was dotted with dead fir trees, standing like skeletons.

"But if we cross it, the Redcoats will see us if they come across the mountain," I said.

"If we go back, we'll hang," Alan said softly.

"It's all a risk," I said. "Let's go ahead."

Alan was delighted.

"Ye're a brave lad, Davie," he said.

We came slowly down the mountain-side and slipped into the heather. For most of the time we crawled from one clump of heather to another, like hunters tracking the deer. It was another hot day and we had no water left in the brandy bottle.

We took it in turns to sleep and to watch for soldiers. But I fell asleep when I was on guard. By the time I woke up, a group of soldiers had already come down the hill-side. They were making their way towards us, spread out in the shape of a fan.

"I've let us down," I whispered to Alan, ashamed.

"What can we do now?"

He pointed to a high mountain ahead of us, to the north-east.

"We'll try to get over to Ben Alder," he said.

"But we'll have to cross right in front of the soldiers!" I said.

"I ken that," he said, "and ye ken that if we turn back to Appin, we're dead men!"

As Alan spoke, he began to run through the heather on his hands and knees. I followed him as quickly as I could. A thin choking dust rose from the ground as we moved, drying our throats even more. Only my fear of letting Alan down again made me carry on.

At dusk, we heard the sound of a trumpet and the soldiers stopped to set up camp in the middle of the moor.

"There'll be no sleep for us tonight!" Alan whispered. "When day comes, we'll be safe on the mountain."

"I can't go on, Alan," I gasped.

"Very well, then, I'll carry ye," Alan said.

"No," I whispered. "Lead the way."

The night was cool and dark. A heavy dew fell and drenched the moor like rain and we wet our lips with it. I thought of nothing else but the next step. And I thought that each one would be my last.

When day dawned, we were far enough away from

the soldiers to walk instead of crawl. But our troubles were not over.

As we walked, four men jumped out of the heather and held their dirks to our throats.

CHAPTER NINE
The Quarrel

Alan whispered to the men in Gaelic and they put away their weapons – but they took ours, too.

"Don't worry," Alan said, "they're Cluny Macpherson's men. He's been one of the leaders of the Jacobite rebellion for years. I thought he was still in France."

The men invited us to visit Cluny's hiding-place, which was perched on the edge of a mountain. He was pleased to see us.

"Bonnie Prince Charlie hid here with me once," he boasted.

It was a long and tiring evening for me. I could not understand a word of the conversation because everybody spoke Gaelic. I soon fell into a deep sleep. I can remember only one thing about that strange evening – Alan lost all our money playing cards. In the morning, Cluny gave it back to us. I did not want it, for I felt that it had been fairly won, but I had to swallow my pride and take it.

Two days later, one of Cluny's men took us across Loch Ericht and on to Loch Rannoch. From there, Alan and I travelled towards the head of the River Forth, in the Lowlands. It was a terrible journey. At night, we crossed high mountains in heavy rain and fierce winds. By day, we lay and slept in the wet heather. It was often misty and we lost our way more than once.

I felt so ill that I wanted to die. And I was so angry with Alan for gambling with our money that we hardly spoke until the third night.

"Let me carry your pack," he said.

"I can carry it, thank you," I said coldly.

"I'll not offer again, David," he said. "I'm not a patient man."

"I never said you were," I answered, as silly and as rude as a boy of ten.

I knew that I was wrong to be so unforgiving, but I could not help it. Then Alan began to whistle a Jacobite tune.

"Just you remember that my king is King George!" I said angrily.

"And I am a Stewart!" he answered, "the same name as my king!"

"I saw many Stewarts while I was in the Highlands," I said, "and they would all be better for a good wash!"

"Do ye know that ye insult me?" Alan asked fiercely.

I pulled out my sword as Alan had taught me. Alan pulled out his sword, too. There was a long silence.

"I cannae fight ye," Alan said at last. He threw his sword onto the ground. "Nae, nae, I cannae."

The anger drained out of me. I felt sick and dizzy and I thought that I was dying.

"I can't breathe properly," I gasped. "If I die, Alan, will you forgive me for what I said?"

Alan picked me up and carried me on his back. We were friends again at last.

CHAPTER TEN
Back to the House of Shaws

For the rest of July and into August, Alan and I travelled on into the Lowlands. I decided that I would go and see Mr Rankeillor in Queensferry. I knew that he was my uncle's lawyer, but I did not know what else to do.

"I should be able to trust him," I told myself. "He's a lawyer. I'll tell him how my uncle had me kidnapped."

At last, I left Alan in hiding to walk into Queensferry. The sun was just coming up. I did not ask the way because I was so ashamed of my dirty appearance. Instead, I walked up and down strange streets, like a dog looking for its master. After a while, I saw a man coming out of a fine tall house. He looked strangely at me.

"What are you doing here, boy?" he asked.

"I'm here on business, sir," I replied. "I'm looking for Mr Rankeillor's house."

"I am Mr Rankeillor," he said.

I took a deep breath to stop myself from trembling.

"My name is David Balfour," I said. "I should like to speak to you in private, sir."

To my relief, Mr Rankeillor did not send me away. He took me into his house and I started to tell him my story.

"The ship sank, sir, and…"

"I heard about the shipwreck," Mr Rankeillor said, "but that was on the 27 June! Today is the 24 August. Where have you been?"

"If I tell you, I shall have to mention a friend."

Mr Rankeillor looked worried.

"Do not mention any Highlander names to me," he said. "Many of them have broken the law. Call your friend…er…Mr Thompson."

How kind Mr Rankeillor was! When I had finished speaking, he fed me and gave me clean clothes. I slowly came back to life.

"I knew your father, David," he said later. "He and your uncle were in love with the same woman – your mother. They came to an agreement. Your father married her and moved to Essendean. Ebenezer kept the family estate, the house of Shaws, near Edinburgh. It is yours now by law."

"But my father was the younger brother," I said in surprise. "Surely it belongs to my uncle?"

"No, David," Mr Rankeillor said. "Your father was the elder brother. You inherit everything on his death. Your uncle knew that."

"So that's why he tried to kill me," I whispered.

"It would be better to settle this matter privately," Mr Rankeillor said. "Otherwise, your friendship with …er…Mr Thompson might be a problem."

I thought about it for a long time.

"Mr Rankeillor," I said at last, "I have an idea…"

It was dark when Alan, Mr Rankeillor, his clerk and myself reached the house of Shaws. No lights shone from its windows, and I shuddered as I remembered the night in June when I came there alone.

Alan walked up to the door and knocked loudly as we hid in the bushes. The window above the door opened with a clatter.

"What's this?" my uncle shouted. "What brings ye here at this time of the night?"

"David," Alan said.

My uncle came to the door slowly, holding a gun.

"I have a friend who lives near the Island of Mull," Alan said. "A ship was wrecked there in June. My friend found a young boy, half-drowned, on the sands – your nephew, David Balfour."

Alan paused and stared at my uncle.

"I've come with a message. Do ye want the lad killed or kept?"

"They'll get no money from me," my uncle shouted.

"Killed or kept?" Alan repeated.

There was a long silence.

"Kept," my uncle muttered. "We'll have naemore bloodshed."

I stepped out of the bushes.

"Good evening, uncle," I said.

And as Mr Rankeillor appeared next to me, my uncle stood clutching his gun like a man turned to stone. We went into the house where my uncle and the lawyer talked late into the night. By the time I went to bed, it was agreed that my uncle would pay me two thirds of his income from the estate of the house of Shaws. I lay until dawn, watching the flames flicker on the ceiling of my room and planning my future now that I was a rich man.

And Alan? He is waiting for a ship to take him to France. I dread him going, for I do not think that I shall ever find such a good friend again.